DISNEY'S
THE NEW ADVENTURES OF
WINNIE the POOH
Stripes

Twin Books

MALLARD PRESS

The rain had just ended in Hundred-Acre Wood and
there were mud puddles everywhere.

We all know mud puddles were made for splashing in.
And that's exactly what Tigger was doing.

"Hoo-Hoo-Hoooo," said Tigger, "there's a good one!" as he
landed in a really big puddle.

Suddenly, Pooh, Piglet and Rabbit ran out from some nearby bushes. Pooh and Rabbit grabbed Tigger by the arms and legs. Piglet grabbed him by the tail.

Rabbit counted "One, two, threeee!" as they hurled Tigger into the air.

Muddy Tigger landed in a great big wooden tub full of water and suds.

"If you're going to bounce in mud puddles, you're going to take baths!" said Rabbit as he ran to the tub of suds, followed by Pooh and Piglet.

And they all began scrubbing Tigger with scrub brushes.

When they were done scrubbing Tigger, Rabbit doused him with a bucket of water to rinse him off.

And when he stepped out of the tub, Tigger was surprised to see that he had no stripes!

"Who are you?" asked Piglet.

"Tigger!" said Tigger. "Who else would I be, for goodness sakes?"

"Why, you couldn't possibly be Tigger," said Rabbit. "Tiggers have stripes!"

"He has two ears and a tail," said Piglet. "Maybe he's a rabbit!"

Tigger stretched his ears.

Then he tugged Rabbit's ears.

"Hey, yeah!" said Tigger. "And Rabbit doesn't have any stripes, either! Maybe I am a rabbit! Wait a minute! I don't know how to be a rabbit! What do I do?"

Rabbit escorted Tigger to his garden to give him his first lesson in being a rabbit.

"The most important thing to a rabbit is his garden," said Rabbit.

"And your first lesson in being a rabbit is to use this pest spray to protect my prize-winning tomatoes. Don't let any pests near them!" warned Rabbit.

"I'll guard your tomatoes as if they were my very own vegebubbles, fellow rabbit!" declared Tigger.

Rabbit left, and Tigger began marching back and forth, guarding the garden.

Suddenly he stopped marching. A noise coming from one of the tomato plants had caught his ear. "Halt! Who crawls there?" yelled Tigger.

It was a hungry little bug.

"Aww…you're hungry, huh, bugsy boy?"

The hungry little bug nodded 'yes.'

"Well, I guess one little tomato wouldn't hurt. Just don't tell the other rabbit, okay?"

And with that, Tigger plucked a nice, juicy tomato and gave it to the hungry little bug.

The bug ate the tomato with one bite!

Just then, Rabbit returned and saw what had happened.

"Oh, no!" he exclaimed. "You didn't! You did!"

"Aw, what's the big deal, fellow rabbit?" said Tigger. "It's just one hungry, defenseless little bug."

"But, you don't understand," said Rabbit. "He'll tell his friends where there's food, and…"

TOMATOE

But it was too late. Rabbit's garden was gone. He and
Tigger stood in the middle of a devastated tomato field.
There were remnants of tomatoes dripping off the vines and
countless bloated, contented, fat little bugs lying around,
digesting.

"Get out!" screamed Rabbit as he chased Tigger out of what used to be his garden. "Get out of here, you pest!"

Tigger ran as fast as he could, with Rabbit right behind him, spraying furiously.

Tigger found a nice tree to lean on as he settled down to catch his breath. Just then he saw Winnie the Pooh chasing a butterfly through the trees.

"Sayyy…I wonder," wondered Tigger, "if I'm a bear!"

Pooh gave Tigger his first lesson in being a bear.

He showed him how to climb a honey tree and get honey out of a beehive.

But Tigger accidentally knocked the hive out of the tree and all the angry bees chased him deep into the woods.

Pooh found Tigger sitting dejectedly under a tree.

"I don't think I want to be a bear," said Tigger. "Maybe I'm a piglet."

So, Pooh and Tigger went to Piglet's house to find out.

After they got there, Tigger tried on some of Piglet's shirts. They were much too small for him. One of Piglet's shirts just barely fit onto one of Tigger's legs.

"I'm afraid you're too big to be a piglet," said Piglet. "We can't all be small animals."

"But the stripes look good on you," said Pooh.

"Heyyy! Maybe I'm a Tigger!" declared Tigger.

"No, I'm afraid there's only one," said Pooh, "and he has stripes."

"Maybe we could paint stripes on him," said Piglet.

So Pooh and Piglet painted stripes on Tigger, and when they were done, Tigger was so happy he started bouncing with joy.

"I'm a Tigger! I'm a Tigger."

He was so happy to have stripes that he bounced right out the door.

Suddenly, there was a loud clap of thunder, and it began to rain.

Tigger's new stripes ran down his body and onto the ground in puddles. Dejected and dripping, Tigger shook his head slowly.

"I'm not a Tigger!"

In the moonlight the rain dripped to a stop.
"I'm not a Tigger...I'm not a Rabbit...I'm not a
bear...and I'm sure not a Piglet," he sniffed.
"I'm not an anything."

Just then Eeyore walked by.

"Hello, Tigger," said Eeyore.

"Hello, Eeyore," answered Tigger.

"Hey! You called me Tigger!"

"Well, aren't you?" asked Eeyore.

"No," said Tigger, "I don't have any stripes!"

"Aw, it doesn't matter. You're still a Tigger on the inside. You'll always be Tigger," said Eeyore.

"Yeahhh-hoooo!!" screamed Tigger, jumping wildly in the air.

Tigger bounced happily around Eeyore, using his tail like a giant spring.

Suddenly, Tigger's tail went out of control, and he landed hard on his bottom.

With a loud "POP!" a stripe popped onto Tigger's tail.
"Yahoo!" yelled Tigger, as he started to bounce even
more.

And as he did so, more and more stripes popped on all
over his body.

Winnie the Pooh, Piglet and Rabbit came out to see what all the noise was about. Tigger came bouncing past them like a Tigger with a mission.

"Now I'm Tigger on the outside and Tigger on the inside, too!"

And as he bounced off into the sunset, he shouted, "And I've got a lot of bouncing to catch up on!"